Autumn Adventure

This musical story shows how much fun
making believe with your friends can be.

Story by:
Phil Baron

Illustrated by:
David High
Russell Hicks
Theresa Mazurek
Julie Ann Armstrong
Allyn Conley-Gorniak

WORLDS OF WONDER™

Worlds of Wonder, Inc. is the exclusive licensee, manufacturer and distributor of The World of Teddy Ruxpin toys.
"The World of Teddy Ruxpin" and "Teddy Ruxpin" are trademarks of Alchemy II, Inc., Chatsworth, CA.
The symbol ₩•₩ and "Worlds of Wonder" are trademarks of Worlds of Wonder, Inc., Fremont, California.

Grubby™ Newton Gimmick™ Princess Aruzia™ Leota™ Wooly What's-It™

Prince Arin™ Fobs®

D1501954

All our friends have to do is look around and listen, to know all about Autumn.

Autumn is another name for Fall.

Do you wonder why the pumpkins only come out in Autumn?

"Let's Make Believe"

Grubby and I helped
Gimmick make a mud
and branch costume.

Wooly was so surprised he ran off and climbed a tree!

Suddenly we saw something real strange.

"Pumpkins on Parade"